leapfrog

Prickly Ballroom

by Ian Smith and Sean Julian

W
FRANKLIN WATTS

First published in 2011 by
Franklin Watts
338 Euston Road
London
NW1 3BH

Franklin Watts Australia
Level 17/207 Kent Street
Sydney
NSW 2000

A CIP catalogue record for this book is available
from the British Library.

ISBN 978 0 7496 9469 2 (hbk)
ISBN 978 0 7496 9475 3 (pbk)

Series Editor: Jackie Hamley
Series Advisor: Catherine Glavina
Series Designer: Peter Scoulding

Printed in China

Franklin Watts is a divison of
Hachette Children's Books,
an Hachette UK company.
www.hachette.co.uk

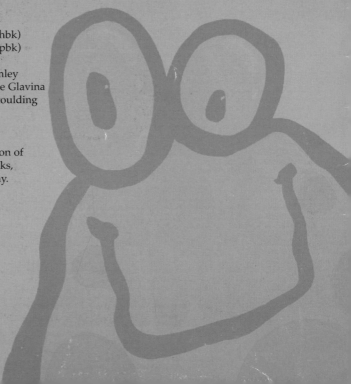

One morning, Porcupine saw a poster for a dance competition.

Porcupine loved
to dance.

He just needed a partner.

But all the animals said, "Sorry, Porcupine, you're too prickly!"

Porcupine was sad.
He wondered what
he could do.

He tried putting on
a thick coat ...

... but his prickles
poked through.

He tried putting corks
on his prickles ...

... but the corks fell off.

Porcupine went to see
Rabbit, the hairdresser.

"No one will dance with me because I'm so prickly. Please cut off my prickles!" he told Rabbit.

Rabbit had a better idea.
"Meet me at the dance
tonight!" she said.

When Porcupine arrived,
all the other animals
were already there.

He was very nervous.

But then Rabbit arrived.
On her paws she wore a
pair of thick oven gloves.

"Brilliant!" laughed Porcupine.

Porcupine and Rabbit
started to dance.

They twirled and twisted.

They jumped and jived.

They spun and shook.

The Judges gave them
first prize.

Porcupine was delighted.
"Thank you, Rabbit!"
he cheered.

Then the animals danced
together all night long ...
with Porcupine!

Puzzle 1

Put these pictures in the correct order.
Now tell the story in your own words.
How short can you make the story?

furious   caring

kind

shy   naughty

nervous

Choose the words which best describe each character. Can you think of any more? Pretend to be one of the characters!

Answers

Puzzle 1

The correct order is:

1e, 2c, 3b, 4f, 5a, 6d

Puzzle 2

Rabbit The correct words are caring, kind.
The incorrect word is furious.

Porcupine The correct words are nervous, shy.
The incorrect word is naughty.

For details of all our titles go to: www.franklinwatts.co.uk

*hardback